MY CAT IS GOING TO THE DOGS

by Mike Thaler • pictures by Jared Lee

MEOW.

Troll Associates

**For Dr. Andre Ross,
who always had
strange things in her icebox!
M.T.**

**To my daughter Jana
who loves animals
J.L.**

Library of Congress Cataloging-in-Publication Data

Thaler, Mike, (date)
    My cat is going to the dogs / by Mike Thaler; pictures by Jared
Lee.
        p.   cm.—(Funny Firsts)
    Summary: A young boy worries about what will happen to his sick
cat when he takes it to the veterinarian for the first time.
    ISBN 0-8167-3022-9 (lib. bdg.)   ISBN 0-8167-3023-7 (pbk.)
    [1. Veterinarians—Fiction.   2. Cats—Fiction.]   I. Lee, Jared
D., ill.   II. Title.   III. Series.
PZ7.T3Mt   1994
[E]—dc20   93-18596

FUNNY FIRSTS™ 1994 Mike Thaler and Jared Lee
Text copyright © 1994 Mike Thaler
Illustrations copyright © 1994 Jared Lee
Published by Troll Associates.

Printed in the United States of America.

10 9 8 7 6 5 4 3 2 1

My cat, Max, is sick.

He got real fat, and doesn't want to play. I didn't know cats got sick just like people.

Do other animals get sick, too? Do weasels get measles?

Do porcupines get pimples?

Do frogs get people in their throats?

Mom says we're taking Max to a veterinarian—a doctor just for animals.

Do the animals sit in the waiting room and read magazines just like we do? Is the nurse an aardvark?

I wonder if the whole zoo will be at the doctor's office. Maybe we'll see an elephant with a cold,

or a giraffe with a sore throat,

or a zebra with a sunburn.

Maybe there will be an alligator with a toothache,

or a big snake with a bellyache.

I wonder if the doctor treats the animals just like people?

I've heard that doctors do experiments on animals.

I won't let him hurt you, Max.

There are no unusual animals in the
waiting room, just a girl with a dog.
The dog looks scared.

Then out comes the nurse.
She's not an aardvark!

They go in and close the door.
Suddenly, there are horrible noises!

Then out they come. The dog's on crutches, and we're next!

We go into the room. There are all sorts of strange things in bottles. Will Max wind up in a bottle?

The doctor comes in. He pats Max on the head. Then he puts on rubber gloves and looks in Max's ears. I wonder what he's looking for?

Then he looks in Max's eyes and in his mouth. I guess he didn't find it in his ears.

Then he listens to Max's heart. I'm getting very nervous. Will Max have to go to the hospital? Will he die?

Then he gently pats Max's stomach and smiles. When he tells us the news, even Max looks surprised.

Guess what? The vet was right.
A week later, Max had four kittens.

So I changed his name to Maxine.

Mom let me keep all the kittens.

And, if they ever get sick, I'm going to take them to my friend . . .

Dr. Beagle, the vet!